THE FOUNTAIN OF YOUTH

THE SHOOTING SCRIPT

AUSTIN PARENTI

NOBLE ROGUE
PUBLISHING

To *The Fountain of Youth* crew,
a remarkable group of creatives
who labored through a South Florida
summer to make this film a reality.

FOREWORD

I pulled up to the Clematis City Docks at 6:30am on June 7, 2021, driving a packed purple mini-van. Dolly tracks poked at my neck the entire drive. I stepped outside and drank in the salty ocean air. A pale white sun peaked over Palm Beach Island, pitching a pink sky. I found our cinematographer, Zach Guinta, and told him: "I dreamed about this all night." He shot me a funny look and replied, "Me too!"

For the next two months, we ventured across Palm Beach County and produced *The Fountain of Youth*. We toured jungles, rivers, beaches, churches, and pancake houses, telling the story of a grand adventure while having our very own. But this wasn't your usual indie film production (not that the word *usual* should ever describe a film production). Of our 17-person crew, 13 were highschoolers.

The Fountain of Youth was an experiment. Could a bunch of highschoolers and their teachers produce something meaningful and beautiful? After 6 months of planning, 42 days of shooting, and 4 months of editing, we premiered the film locally and online. To date, the film has over 100,000 views and won two Silver Tellys, a Platinum Viddy, and a Gold AVA Digital Award.

I smile when I think of The Fountain of Youth, not because of the accolades, but because of the crew. The faculty (Zach Guinta, Tim DeMoss, and Philip King) set a tone of perseverance and patience. They pulled double duties, not only doing their own jobs with tremendous skill, but teaching students how to do theirs.

Those 13 highschoolers were among the most exceptional people I've ever met. They were extremely mature, smart, and disciplined. Their intense willingness to carry a 500-pound fountain half a mile through the woods was rivaled only by their brilliant creativity. It was an honor laboring alongside them, and I am forever grateful for their grit and determination in the summer of 2021.

Sincerely yours,

Austin Parenti

<u>THE FOUNTAIN OF YOUTH</u>

Written by

Austin Parenti

1   EXT. HEART OF JUNGLE - DAWN (1521)   1

A jungle.

A MAN.

He wears a green shirt, dirtied trousers, and... a metal
breastplate? A pointy helmet? A conquistador! This must be
JUAN PONCE DE LEON.

Stabbing his cane and boots into the ground, he treks through
the wild, swatting branches and flies. MAGICAL, WONDEROUS
music plays as Ponce de Leon parts a palm frond, revealing:

THE FOUNTAIN--a simple stone pillar pumps water out its peak
and into a pond below. Haze rises from the dewy ground and
wraps around a figure, the GUARDIAN.

Ponce De Leon smiles. He's never been happier, nor more
relieved. He approaches the Guardian and bows low. From a
distance, we watch them exchange words and gestures.

The Guardian produces a flagon. He dips it in the fountain's
greatest bowl and hands it to Ponce. CLOSE ON Ponce as he
stares at the shimmering cup.

                    TEACHER (V.O.)
              Ponce De Leon was the greatest
              explorer in Florida history.

2   INT. ELEMENTARY CLASSROOM - DAY (2001)   2

CLOSE ON ASHER, a young boy. He sits silently among other
rowdy children.

                    TEACHER
              ... And we have a guest speaker to
              tell us all about him!

Asher and his classmates perk up and look around, excited.

                    TEACHER (CONT'D)
              He's someone you might recognize
              from TV. A real life explorer...
              Let me introduce our hometown hero,
              Mr. Giacomo Tonti!

GIACOMO TONTI, 40's, a slightly dishevled, lazy "explorer"
nonchalantly enters the class.

                    GIACOMO
              Hello.

                            2

Kids point and cheer for their hero.

                    GIACOMO (CONT'D)
            (to Teacher; a murmur)
      You have the, uh...

He holds out his index and middle fingers, rubbing both with
his thumb.

                    TEACHER
      Oh, yes.

The Teacher withdraws an envelope and hands it to Giacomo,
who smiles and stashes his check. He turns back to the class.

                    GIACOMO
            (a bit awkward; out of his
             element)
      I'm Giacomo Tonti. You've probably
      seen my show. Been all over the
      world. Seen a lot of weird stuff.

Asher is absolutely star struck. It's like he's staring at
Iron Man himself.

                    GIACOMO (CONT'D)
      Florida's a great place though.
      Tons to see here, too. The girls
      are great.

He chuckles to himself. The Teacher intentionally clears her
throat.

                    TEACHER
            (on cue)
      Who inspired you, Mr. Tonti?

                    GIACOMO
            (catching the cue)
      Right. Well that would be the
      <u>bravest</u> explorer in Florida
      History. Juan Ponce de Leon.

Giacomo approaches a portrait of the hanging on the wall. The
class OOHS and AAHS.

                    GIACOMO (CONT'D)
            (getting into it now)
      This Spaniard braved snakes,
      natives, and gators all in search
      of gold and glory. But some think
      there was more to his quest then
      that.

Asher tilts his head, "huh?"

> GIACOMO (CONT'D)
> Ponce de Leon believed in a magical
> pond. If you drank its water, you
> would live forever. <u>The Fountain of</u>
> <u>Youth</u>. Just imagine if you found
> this place: No more death.

CLOSE ON Asher, his eyes wide with wonder.

3   EXT. BACKYARD - DAY   3

Through a magnifying glass, we see the warped face of SEAN,
Asher's best friend. He's crouched over studying a plant. He
glances at his field journal.

> SEAN
> (with much effort)
> "Rhododendron Austrinum." Florida's
> Flame Azalea. Poisonous to eat, but
> not to touch.

Asher appears with a walking stick and marches around Sean.

> ASHER
> We just learned about a fountain
> that'll make you live forever, and
> all you wanna do is look at a
> flower!

> SEAN
> A poisonous flower.

> ASHER
> It could still be out there.

> SEAN
> My dad says it's fake. What does
> your dad think?

Asher looks down, sulking.

> ASHER
> Well...

MRS. JUNE, Asher's mother, enters the yard.

> MRS. JUNE
> Asher, Sean, no more playing. Time
> for dinner.

Asher and Sean walk toward the house.

> ASHER
> Just think about it Sean--we could
> be the ones to find it!

> SEAN
> We'd need to do lots of planning.
> Snacks, sleeping bags, my field
> guide. We wouldn't wanna end up
> like Pon... Ponce...

Asher jumps on a stump for dramatic effect.

> ASHER
> Ponce de Leon! The greatest
> explorer in Florida history.

CLOSE ON ASHER, eyes widened.

4   INT. HIGHSCHOOL CLASSROOM - DAY (2021)   4

CLOSE ON ASHER, still with widened eyes, but now he's 24 and
a teacher.

> ASHER
> Can you imagine this man's courage?
> Braving the swamps and storms of
> South Florida, only for what? Some
> money and fame? No, he wanted more.
> He wanted life. And he wanted it
> forever! Now, most people think the
> fountain is just a myth. But what
> if it's not? What if you found it?
> Would you drink it?

REVEAL: His STUDENTS, sleeping, bored, yawning.

Asher's smile fades. But a student in the back raises her
hand!

> ASHER (CONT'D)
> Yes, Anna!

> ANNA
> Can I go to the bathroom?

His smile fades again. He gestures to dismiss her.

> ASHER
> Come on, guys! We're talking about
> everlasting life. Really think
> about it. Is that something you
> would want?
> (MORE)

5

                    ASHER (CONT'D)
          To live in this world forever?
          Would you drink from the fountain?

No one responds. So Asher picks on someone at random:

                    ASHER (CONT'D)
          Cody.

CODY shrugs his shoulders, clearly not caring.

                    CODY
          Would you?

Asher thinks. He's about to answer when the BELL RINGS. The
class starts to leave.

                    ASHER
          Chapters 6 and 7 homework due
          Tuesday, enjoy the long weekend!

5   INT. SCHOOL HALLWAY - DAY   5

Asher leaves his classroom and spots the PRINCIPAL, walking
down the hall.

                    ASHER
          Miss Brown!

Asher catches up to her as she deeply exhales, getting ready
for a conversation she doesn't want to have. They continue to
walk.

                    ASHER (CONT'D)
          Have you thought about my idea?

                    PRINCIPAL
          We already have a history club.

                    ASHER
          Well, archaeology is pretty
          different from history--

                    PRINCIPAL
          Would students really want to join
          something like that?

                    ASHER
          Of course! We'd go on field trips
          to dig sites and--

                    PRINCIPAL
          You want to take students to South
          America?!

> ASHER
> No, no! Local. You'd be surprised
> how much of South Florida hasn't
> been explored.

> PRINCIPAL
> Still, we're talking about
> transportation, parent permission
> slips... you're asking a lot,
> Asher.

Asher steps in front of the Principal to stop her for a
moment.

> ASHER
> Miss Brown, I can't teach my
> students history--<u>real history</u>--on
> a white board.

> PRINCIPAL
> Why not? That's what every teacher
> does around the world.

> ASHER
> But--

> PRINCIPAL
> It's a no, Asher.

She walks away, leaving Asher standing in defeat.

6   INT. ASHER'S APARTMENT - NIGHT   6

Asher enters the dark apartment, but when he flips on the
lights, he's shocked by a loud, "SURPRISE".

Three people stand in the living room, beneath a Happy
Birthday banner:

First, Sean, now 25 and wearing a paramedic's uniform.
Second, Mrs. June, older and with a walker--she's not well,
but still tries to appear her blunt and usual self. Third,
there is VAL (20's), an awkward but gruff Atlanta gal.

Asher lets out a hardly noticeable sigh.

7   INT. ASHER'S APARTMENT - LATER   7

The four sit around a table, eating cake. Slowly. Awkwardly.

Mrs. June unconciously taps on a MYSTERIOUS LETTER.

                    MRS. JUNE
          So... 25 years old. Thought of any
          resolutions?

She eyes Val.

                    ASHER
          Actually, yes! I applied to grad
          school. There's this archaeology
          college--

                    VAL
          Wowza, ain't that something.

She's so into him.

                    ASHER
          Right...

He's so not into her.

                    MRS. JUNE
               (not excited)
          Where is it?

                    ASHER
          London.

Dead stop.

Mrs. June looks down, disappointed with him. She quietly
slides the Mysterious Letter off the table and into her
purse.

                    VAL
          Sure you'd want to be away from
          your students for that long?

                    ASHER
          Oh, I'm sure.

                    MRS. JUNE
               (cynically)
          C'mon Val, we hardly see him as is.
          What's another few thousand miles?

                    VAL
          Sean--won't you miss him?

                    SEAN
               (sarcastic)
          Hardly.

                        VAL
            Shouldn't he stay?

Sean shrugs.

                        SEAN
            He's too stupid to listen to me,
            anyway.

                        ASHER
            Look, I'm not married, I have no
            commitments; this might be the only
            time I can try something like this!

He takes a bite of his cake.

                        ASHER (CONT'D)
                (mouth full of cake)
            And it's my birthday, you should
            all be happy for me.

He stuffs a big bite of cake in his face. The others stay
silent.

INT. ASHER'S APARTMENT - LATER   8

Asher waves out the door as Sean leaves. Val leaves too, but
waits a moment.

                        VAL
            You coming, Miss June?

                        MRS. JUNE
            Give us a moment, Val.

Val steps away. Asher closes the door and breathes in,
bracing himself. Mrs. June is smug and blunt, but there is
something charming about her wit and tough-love.

                        MRS. JUNE (CONT'D)
            Well that was a disaster.

                        ASHER
         Mom...

                        MRS. JUNE
             You used to have so many friends.
            Now I can barely find two to show
            up and surprise you.

                        ASHER
            It's hard to stay in touch with--

                    MRS. JUNE
          Sean traded a shift at the hospital
          to be here. Did you thank him?

                    ASHER
          Yes, Mom--

                    MRS. JUNE
          --And poor Valerie! She told me you
          don't take her calls.

                    ASHER
          Ma: we went on, like, two dates and
          she was already acting like we're
          married!

                    MRS. JUNE
          Would that be the worst thing in
          the world?

                    ASHER
          Maybe! She goes shooting on
          weekends. She's... weird, Ma.

                    MRS. JUNE
          I don't know what she sees in you.
          Kind girl like that deserves
          better.

Asher smiles, amused by his mom. He shakes his head.

                    ASHER
          How are you feeling?

                    MRS. JUNE
               (sarcastic)
          Same as I look. A goddess in human
          form.

                    ASHER
          No updates?

                    MRS. JUNE
          Doctors say I've got time and
          plenty of it.

Mrs. June moves with her walker toward the door, but stops
and sighs. She pulls out a MYSTERIOUS LETTER from her purse.

                    MRS. JUNE (CONT'D)
          Here.

                    ASHER
          What is this?

10

> MRS. JUNE
> It was with you the day we adopted
> you. And the nuns said it was with
> you the day they found you.

INSERT - ENVELOPE

"DO NOT OPEN UNTIL YOU TURN 25"

BACK TO SCENE

> ASHER
> Oh my gosh...

He begins to open it; the seal's already broken.

> ASHER (CONT'D)
> Did you open this?

> MRS. JUNE
> Of course I did! Opened it that
> very day.

Asher pulls out a slip of paper as Mrs. June exits.

INSERT - SLIP OF PAPER

"250 S APOXEE TRAIL" followed by the initials "JT"

FADE TO:

9   EXT. GRAVEYARD - NIGHT   9

THUNDER. Haze. A rickety sign that reads "250." Two
flashlights beam across the yard.

Asher and Sean search the graveyard, reading headstones and
looking between forked trees.

> SEAN
> I gotta be home by nine. I told
> Lori we were bowling.

> ASHER
> Why?

> SEAN
> How was I supposed to explain this?

They come to two long rows of gravestones.

                    SEAN (CONT'D)
          So that note is from your birth
          parents?

                    ASHER
          Maybe. Or it's <u>about</u> my parents.

                    SEAN
          Hey, over here!

Asher joins Sean by a gravestone.

                    SEAN (CONT'D)
          You're not going to like this.

He flashes his light at the gravestone: ASHER NELL - 1960-
2001.

                    ASHER
          Why not?

                    SEAN
          Maybe this is your Dad... he's got
          your name.

                    ASHER
          My <u>adopted parents</u> gave me my name.

                    SEAN
          Oh.

                    ASHER
          Maybe we should dig it up just to
          be certain.

                    SEAN
          Are you crazy?

A shadowy FIGURE quietly approaches from behind.

                    ASHER
          You got a better idea?

                    SEAN
          Yes: To not go to prison!

Suddenly, the sound of a SHOTGUN-COCK startles the boys.
Holding the gun is the figure: FRIAR PETE, the sexton.

                    FRIAR PETE
          Don't you boys have any respect for
          the dead?

                        ASHER
                 (stumbling; afraid)
          I have a letter! It told me to come
          here.

He hands over the letter. Friar Pete reads it, then his tense
expression fades...

10   INT. ABBEY - NIGHT   10

Asher and Sean sit in a dimly-lit room as Friar Pete puts
away his shotgun and rummages through his bookshelves.

                        SEAN
          So... I didn't think ya'll used
          guns.

                        FRIAR PETE
          I'm from Miami.

                        SEAN
          Oh.

                        FRIAR PETE
          Ah, here it is.

He pulls a small, dusty package off a shelf and sits with the
boys.

                        FRIAR PETE (CONT'D)
          It was twenty-five years ago. An
          older gent gave this to me--asked
          me to hold it for a quarter
          century... until someone came back
          for it with a note in his writing,
          with those initials. JT.

He hands the package to Asher.

                        ASHER
          You never opened it?

                        FRIAR PETE
          He made me vow.

                        SEAN
          That's a hard vow to keep!

                        FRIAR PETE
          I've got some practice.

Slowly, Asher opens the package, revealing a large parchment.

Asher's eyes pore over the paper.

> SEAN
> What is it?

Asher goes from focused, to confused, to shocked...

> SEAN (CONT'D)
> What is it?!

Sean and Friar Pete crowd behind Asher.

> ASHER
> It's a map. Listen--the ending:
> "... Press through the underbrush
> till you come to a misty clearing.
> Here you will find the
> Conquistador's treasure; eternal
> waters--the ageless wonder."

Asher puts down the parchment.

> ASHER (CONT'D)
> The Fountain of Youth.

> SEAN
> It doesn't say that.

Sean snatches the parchment.

> ASHER
> It doesn't have to.

> SEAN
> This isn't a map to the Fountain of
> Youth!

> ASHER
> What else could it be?

> SEAN
> A prank. A very elaborate prank.

Sean tosses the paper to Asher.

> ASHER
> My mom would have to be in on it.
> He'd have to be in on it!

Asher points to Friar Pete, who's taking a seat.

Asher looks over the parchment's title line, which reads,
"MIZPAH."

                    ASHER (CONT'D)
What's Mizpah?

                    FRIAR PETE
It's Hebrew. Means 'Watchtower'.

                    ASHER
Maybe a lighthouse?

                    SEAN
Asher, if this was a map to the
fountain, why would it be written
in Hebrew?!

                    ASHER
Maybe the author's religious. Ponce
de Leon was Catholic, right?

                    SEAN
But that paper's only twenty-five
years old!

                    ASHER
Yeah, that's when he received it,
but it could be older. It looks
older...

                    SEAN
     (to Friar Pete)
Can you talk some sense into him?

                    FRIAR PETE
It does seem unlikely. But there is
still a mystery, here. Who made
this map? And why? And why do they
want you to follow it? It may be
worth pursuing if only to learn the
truth.

                    ASHER
Thank you.

                    FRIAR PETE
But this fountain... if I recall,
its legends come from pagan
cultures. If it does exist, it is
not from God. And I don't think He
is pleased when we search for
miracles apart from him.

                    ASHER
Well I would just like to find it.
I wouldn't drink from it, just
discover it.

                    FRIAR PETE
          Even so, be cautious. Those who go
          on these sorts of quests seldom
          return... unchanged.

11   EXT. PARKING GARAGE ROOF - NIGHT   11

ASHER and SEAN sit on a ledge overlooking West Palm Beach.

                    SEAN
          Well, that was pretty weird.

                    ASHER
          I have to do this. Sean, I've
          dreamed of the fountain since I was
          a kid. Obsessed.

                    SEAN
          I know.

                    ASHER
          And the odds of this just dropping
          on my lap!

                    SEAN
          It's a little convenient, don't you
          think?

                    ASHER
          C'mon Sean. If we left in the
          morning, it'd be like a roadtrip.
          Nothing major! Sean? C'mon... boys
          trip?

                    SEAN
          Take a few days and think about it.
          Look over the map. If it really
          seems legit, let's block out a
          weekend. Maybe over Summer break or
          something.

                    ASHER
          You want me to wait three months to
          pursue my dreams?

His phone buzzes.

                    ASHER (CONT'D)
          Oh no.

12   INT. HOSPITAL ROOM - NIGHT   12

Asher and Sean stand in the doorway. Mrs. June lies on the
cot, hooked up to an IV bag.

> MRS. JUNE
> Oh, come in already! Don't stand
> there looking all pathetic.

They draw into the room. Asher sits by her bedside while Sean
evaluates the IV.

> SEAN
> They gotta change this soon. Let me
> find a Nurse.

He steps out.

> ASHER
> What happened?

> MRS. JUNE
> Nothing unexpected.

> ASHER
> But you said--

> MRS. JUNE
> Yes, I've got plenty of time! Weeks
> they say. At best.

In spite of everything, she's solid as a rock.

> ASHER
> Mom... I think I can save you. That
> note you gave me. It might lead to
> the Fountain of Youth.

Mrs. June looks at her son, amused. But she reads his
expression.

> MRS. JUNE
> Alright then, off you go to save
> me.

She waves to dismiss him.

> ASHER
> I'm serious. Think about it, the
> timing of everything. Maybe it's
> fate or something.

                    MRS. JUNE
          The only things fated are "death
          and taxes," -Benjamin Franklin.

                    ASHER
          If there's even the smallest chance
          of it being real, it's worth a
          shot, right?

                    MRS. JUNE
          Asher, what makes you think I'm
          opposed to what's happening to me?

Asher's taken aback.

                    MRS. JUNE (CONT'D)
          We're all given some time and
          sooner or later it's used up. No
          sense in fighting it. Your father
          learned that lesson.

Asher winces at the memory.

                    MRS. JUNE (CONT'D)
          Besides, I'd much rather have you
          here. Who else can I make fun of so
          easily?

13   INT. ASHER'S BEDROOM - NIGHT   13

Asher looks the map over again and again. Eventually, he puts
it down.

His eyes drift to his bookshelf. Adventure stories pack its
slim shelves, everything from the Odyssey to Treasure Island
and Jules Verne.

HOPEFUL MUSIC builds.

Asher's eyes rest on a family photo: him and his adopted
parents. He looks determined.

14   EXT. SEAN'S HOUSE - DAY   14

Through a magnifying glass, we see the warped face of Sean
again. He and his son TIMMY, 4-6, are crouched over, studying
a plant in the front yard.

                    SEAN
          What do you think?

Sean's son flips through his father's field guide.

> TIMMY
> (with much effort)
> Callicarpa Americana. Edible.

Suddenly, a car pulls up and shrieks to a halt. Asher gets out, holding the map.

> SEAN
> Gimme a minute, Timmy.

Timmy scurries into the house as Asher marches right up to Sean.

> SEAN (CONT'D)
> Is your mom alright?

> ASHER
> No. Most people, when stuff like
> this happens, there's nothing they
> can do. Now I don't know if it's
> fate or chance or a prank, but
> we've got something right here that
> might make a difference. Don't do
> this for me. Do it for her. Look
> man, I need your help. I can't do
> this without you.

Sean smiles. He can't believe what he's about to do.

> SEAN
> We need a plan. And snacks.

15   EXT. ASHER'S CAR - DAY   15

Sean paces with a clipboard and his field guide as Asher inspects items in the trunk of his car.

> SEAN
> Toiletries.

> ASHER
> Check.

> SEAN
> First aid.

> ASHER
> Check.

SEAN'S WIFE brings over two sleeping bags and tosses them in the trunk.

                    SEAN
          Sleeping bags.

                    ASHER
          Check.

                    SEAN'S WIFE
               (Asher)
          Keep him safe, you hear?

                    ASHER
          Yes 'mam.

She exits.

                    SEAN
          Field guide.

Asher looks around the trunk, not seeing it. Sean realizes
it's in his hands. He tosses it in the trunk.

                    SEAN (CONT'D)
          Check.

Asher slams the trunk shut.

16   INT. ASHER'S CAR - DAY   16

Asher and Sean enter the car.

                    SEAN
          So where to?

                    ASHER
          Oh. Right.

Asher pulls out the map and studies it. He sighs in
frustration.

                    SEAN
          The Hebrew part?

                    ASHER
          Mizpah. If it's talking about a
          lighthouse, there's dozens in
          Florida.

Sean points to the map's edge.

                    SEAN
          What about that?

INSERT - MAP

The initials "JT" sit at the bottom right of the parchment.

BACK TO SCENE.

                      SEAN (CONT'D)
      JT.

Asher shrugs.

                      ASHER
      Not sure. Could be a name.

                      SEAN
      Can we skip the Hebrew for now?

                      ASHER
      I tried, but it goes straight into
      the first clue, and I have no idea
      where it is.

Sean takes the map from Asher.

                      SEAN
      "Climb the Queen's tower, then be
      Prudent." A casino?

                      ASHER
      What?

                      SEAN
      You know, cards... queen, king,
      ace?

                      ASHER
      Doubt it.

                      SEAN
      So we've got a watchtower, then a
      queen's tower. Who in the world
      would know what this stuff means?

Asher has an idea.

17   EXT. RANCH - DAY   17

Asher knocks on the front door.

                      MAN'S VOICE (O.S.)
      What?

Sean looks at Asher. Asher returns a reassuring look. He
knocks again.

                         MAN'S VOICE (O.S.) (CONT'D)
          What?!

At this point, the sloppily dressed, poorly groomed man has
opened the door, revealing himself to be...

                    SEAN
          Giacomo Tonti?

                    ASHER
          Mr. Tonti! I started your fan club
          chapter at Palm Beach High--do you
          remember me?

Giacomo Tonti looks Asher up and down.

                    GIACOMO
          No?

                    ASHER
          Sir, we need your help with
          something. My mom's really sick and
          we think this could help her.

Asher holds out the old map. Giacomo looks at the map
intently.

18   INT. RANCH LIVING ROOM - DAY   18

Asher and Sean sit in Giacomo's dusty living room. It's
filled with old adventure memorabilia, medals, etc.

Asher can't help but take a few photos on his phone. Giacomo
enters with a tray of tea mugs, catching Asher in the act.
Asher puts the phone on the coffee table.

                    SEAN
          Quite the place you've got here.
          Lots of medals.

Giacomo scoffs.

                    GIACOMO
          They're nothing. Bunch of local
          crap. You don't get big unless you
          do something big.

                    SEAN
          But you had a TV show.

                    GIACOMO
          Heh, oh yeah. Cancelled after one
          season.

                    ASHER
What happened?

                    GIACOMO
They caught me smoking around back.

                    SEAN
What?

                    GIACOMO
It was the 80's. Alright, what do
you got for me?

Asher hands it to Giacomo who studies it closely.

                    ASHER
It's at least twenty-five years
old. We think it may lead us to--

                    GIACOMO
The fountain.

A very subtle hunger has awoken in Giacomo. He keeps scouring
the map.

                    ASHER
This top line is Hebrew for
watchtower.

                    SEAN
And there's a ton of lighthouses in
Florida. Where do we start?

                    GIACOMO
It's not talking about watchtowers,
it's talking about a ship!

Asher and Sean look at each other.

                                CUT TO:

19   INT. RANCH LIVING ROOM - MOMENTS LATER   19

Giacomo slaps down a thick coffee table book on Florida
sunken ships. He thumbs through a few pages until...

                    GIACOMO
Here. The USS Mizpah--naval patrol
yacht scuttled in 1968 off of Palm
Beach.

> SEAN
> What about the first line, "Climb
> the Queens Tower."

> GIACOMO
> Might be part of the ship. But we
> know the next clue is down there.

He points to a photo of the submerged ship, resting quietly
in a world of cold and blue.

> SEAN
> Well, we clearly came to the right
> guy.

> ASHER
> Now all we gotta do is solve the
> other clues and the fountain's
> ours.

Giacomo looks at his guests. He's changed somehow. He seems
lighter, more energized, but something's off...

> GIACOMO
> Let me see the map. "Climb the
> Queen's Tower, then be Prudent."
> You know what? I think I have
> something that could help us. Come!

The boys follow Giacomo out of the room.

CLOSE ON: Asher's phone, still on the coffee table.

20   INT. RANCH ADJACENT ROOM - DAY   20

Giacomo holds the door open for Asher and Sean. Once they
enter, Giacomo slams the door shut and locks it.

Asher and Sean try to reopen it! They start SHOUTING and
BANGING.

> ASHER
> Hey! Hey!!! What are you doing to
> us?!

> GIACOMO
>   (laughing; to himself)
> Idiots.

Giacomo leaves. Asher and Sean SHOUT and BANG some more but
realize it's futile.

                    ASHER
          There's got to be another way out.

                    SEAN
          No windows.

                    ASHER
          Phones!

Asher checks his pockets.

                    SEAN
          In the car. Yours?

                    ASHER
          I left it on the coffee table.

Another idea. He approaches the door and calls out.

                    ASHER (CONT'D)
          Hey Cell Phone!

21 INT. RANCH LIVING ROOM - DAY   21

The Cell Phone BLINKS and CHIRPS--its voice recognition hears
Asher.

22 INT. RANCH ADJACENT ROOM - DAY   22

                    ASHER
          Call 9-1-1. Okay?

23 INT. RANCH LIVING ROOM - DAY   23

                    ASHER (O.S.)
                 (very muffled)
          Call 9-1-1!

                    CELL PHONE
          Calling "Grand-Mama"

It rings. Then:

                    GRANDMA (V.O.)
          Hello? Asher? Hello??

24 INT. RANCH ADJACENT ROOM - DAY   24

Asher rolls his eyes.

                         ASHER
                Grandma, it's Asher!

25   INT. RANCH LIVING ROOM - DAY   25

                         ASHER (O.S.)
                       (very muffled)
                We've been kidnapped, call 9-1-1!

                         GRANDMA (V.O.)
                I can't hear you, sweetie. Call me
                when you have better reception.

        She hangs up.

26   INT. RANCH ADJACENT ROOM - DAY   26

                         ASHER
                Now what?

                         SEAN
                Hey Cell Phone! Call Valerie. VAL-
                ER-IE.

                         ASHER
                What are you thinking? Not her!

                         SEAN
                She lives nearby! You want a shot
                at catching Giacomo or not?

27   INT. RANCH LIVING ROOM - DAY   27

        CLOSE ON Asher's Phone.

                         CELL PHONE
                Calling Valerie.

        It rings. It rings. Finally, she picks up.

                         VAL (V.O.)
                Hello?

                                              CUT TO:

28   EXT. RANCH - DAY   28

        ACTION MUSIC. SLOW MOTION.

Val's rides up on her bicycle. She steps off, wearing aviators, a rifle, and an axe.

She comes to the front door. SMASH. CRASH. BANG.

She enters the ranch as its alarm sounds.

Hold on the exterior of the house. More SMASHING and CRASHING from within.

Finally, Asher, Sean, and Val emerge in a mad rush.

> SEAN
> That was amazing!

> ASHER
> Thank you, thank you, thank you!

> VAL
> What's all this about?

> SEAN
> Giacomo Tonti stole our treasure
> map, we've gotta catch him!

> ASHER
> We'll explain later.

> SEAN
> We owe you one!

29   INT. ASHER'S CAR - DAY   29

Asher and Sean pile in the front seats.

Val enters the back seat.

Asher and Sean are very confused. Val is oblivious.

> ASHER
> Umm, Val?

> VAL
> Yes?

> ASHER
> This might get a little
> dangerous...

> VAL
> Oh! Sorry.

She buckles her seatbelt.

                        VAL (CONT'D)
          Better?

Asher looks to Sean, who is very amused by this. Asher's
about to speak when he hears police sirens nearby.

                        ASHER
          Better.

He presses on the gas.

30   EXT. RANCH - DAY   30

      Asher's car speeds away from the ranch.

31   INT. ASHER'S CAR - LATER   31

                        VAL
          You think it was a map to the
          Fountain of Youth?

                        ASHER
          I know it was.

                        VAL
          Wowza. Well, how are we gonna catch
          him?

               RON   ASHER
          Mizpah!   Mizpah!

                        VAL
          God bless you.

                        SEAN
          Thank you.

32   EXT. DOCKS - DAY   32

      Asher, Sean, and Val rush down the Clematis Street Docks of
      West Palm Beach. Sailors busily march up and down, carrying
      crates, fishing rods, and other boating equipment.

      Asher leads his team through the thick crowd. He's searching
      for someone.

                        SEAN
          So you're good to dive down there
          alone, yeah?

                    ASHER
          No, you're coming with me.

                    SEAN
          I'm not certified!

                    ASHER
          You've been diving before.

                    SEAN
          Yeah, a few classes. But never this
          deep!

                    ASHER
          You'll be fine.

                    VAL
          You thinking we just hire a random
          boat to take ya'll out there?

                    ASHER
          Not a random one.

They come to a grizzly-looking sailor, PAULY, hacking a fish
in two with his machete.

                    ASHER (CONT'D)
          Pauly!

Pauly turns about and sees Asher. His expression remains
sour.

                    PAULY
          Come to pay your debt?

                    ASHER
             (lying)
          What debt?

                    PAULY
          Last time I took you out, you lost
          my speargun!

                    ASHER
          A shark spooked me and I dropped
          it.

                    SEAN
          A shark?!

                    PAULY
          It was my brother's!

                    ASHER
          How was I supposed to know that?

                    PAULY
          So where's my money? You owe me one-
          fifty.

                    ASHER
          Look, we're in a bit of a crisis.
          We've gotta explore the Mizpah
          wreck.

Asher takes out his wallet and pulls out a few bills.

                    ASHER (CONT'D)
          I've got fifty bucks. Can you take
          us there? With tanks and all?

                    PAULY
          That'll barely cover your oxygen.

                    ASHER
          I promise I'll pay you back. For
          the speargun, too.

Pauly thinks it over, looking at the money. He sighs.

33   EXT. PAULY'S BOAT - DOCKED - DAY   33

Pauly's boat is a simple, twenty-foot fishing craft. He loads
his ship with supplies from the dock: scuba tanks, wet suits,
and gas.

Asher and Sean board the ship, but Val stays on the dock.

                    SEAN
          You coming, Val?

                    VAL
          Eh, I'm good. Ya'll let me know
          when you get back.

                    SEAN
          Afraid to get wet?

                    VAL
          I don't do well in boats.

                    ASHER
             (lying)
          Well, that's too bad. Stay safe!

The boat pulls away from the dock. Val watches as they drive out, into the crowded intracoastal waterway.

34   EXT. OCEAN - DAY   34

Pauly's boat speeds across the water, passing through the narrow waterway. It passes Peanut Island and the historic JFK family mansion.

Finally, it emerges from the Palm Beach Inlet into the massive, mysterious blue ocean.

35   EXT. DIVE SITE - DAY   35

Pauly's ship arrives at the dive site. As Asher and Sean glance about the blue waves, they take in an ominous site: another ship. It's empty and anchored less than a hundred feet away.

                    SEAN
          That's gotta be Giacomo.

                    ASHER
          It's a popular spot--might not be
          him.

Pauly approaches.

                    PAULY
          Giacomo Tonti?

                    ASHER
          Yeah. Our competitor.

                    PAULY
          This some kinda race?

                    SEAN
          Yeah. And he locked us in his
          house.

                    PAULY
          Sounds like I'd like him.

                    SEAN
          Let's wait for him to come back up--
          then we can get the map back.

                    ASHER
          What if it's not him and he's on
          his way? Or if he already left?
                    (MORE)

31

                    ASHER (CONT'D)
          We can't waste any time, we've
          gotta get down there now.

                    PAULY
          What's this race all about?

                    ASHER
          Did I pay you to ask questions?

Pauly frowns.

36   EXT. DIVE SITE - MOMENTS LATER   36

Asher and Sean finish equipping their wetsuits, scuba tanks,
and other gear.

Sean sits on the edge of the boat with his feet dangling over
the water.

                    SEAN
          I'm not sure about this.

                    ASHER
          Sean--you're gonna be okay. Just
          remember three things.

                    SEAN
          Three things.

                    ASHER
          One, don't ever hold your breathe.
          Breathe slow and steady.

                    SEAN
          Breathe. Got it.

                    ASHER
          Two, if you panic, <u>don't swim up to
          the surface.</u> Find me and we'll
          decompress together. Slowly.

                    SEAN
          Okay.

                    ASHER
          Lastly, we've got oxygen for two
          hours.

Asher looks at his dive-watch.

                    PAULY
          More like twenty minutes.

                         ASHER
              What?!

                         PAULY
              You gave me fifty bucks. You
              expected full tanks, too?

Asher rolls his eyes and looks back to his watch.

                         ASHER
              It's 3:20 now. We've gotta head
              back up at 3:45 latest for
              decompression.

                         SEAN
              Right. The bends.

                         ASHER
              Just stick close to me. Oh, and we
              gotta watch out for Giacomo.

                         SEAN
              I'm gonna die.

                         ASHER
              You won't die. Probably.

                         SEAN
              What?!

Asher rolls his eyes and shoves Sean off the boat. Then he
puts on his goggles and breather and slides into the water.

37   EXT. UNDERWATER - DAY   37

The silence of the endless, blue expanse is unnerving.

Asher swims up to Sean, who's getting situated in the new
element. Sean gives Asher a thumbs up.

Asher points to his watch and waves for Sean to follow him.

They slowly glide through the sea, away from Pauly's boat.
They descend deeper and deeper; the water around them turns a
darker hue of blue.

All we hear is their steady breathing and the stream of
bubbles breaking from their suits.

38   EXT. UNDERWATER - THE MIZPAH WRECK - CONTINUOUS   38

Something's out there. Something big.

A large silhouette dominates the frame. As Asher and Sean swim closer, the haze fades and we take in the full scale of the Mizpah.

The ship drips with coral and algae. Groupers, baracuda, and other large fish swirl around the sunken vessel.

Asher swims confidently toward the vessel and Sean begrugingly follows.

As they near the ship, Sean looks all around himself. He spots a SHARK swimming slowly by.

Meanwhile, Asher easily swims closer and closer to the Mizpah.

They drift up the side of the ship and come to its top deck. They look around and see no one.

39   EXT. DIVE SITE - DAY   39

A scuba diver emerges above the waves. He takes off his goggles, revealing himself to be Giacomo Tonti.

He swims to his boat and climbs aboard, but spots Pauly, watching from his ship.

Pauly gives Giacomo a curtious wave.

                    PAULY
            You part of the race?

Giacomo looks to Pauly, then back to the water.

                    GIACOMO
            Yeah. And I'll give you a thousand
            dollars to leave them here.

Pauly thinks it over.

                    PAULY
            Show me the money.

40   INT. UNDERWATER - THE MIZPAH WRECK - DAY   40

Asher and Sean explore the inside of the wrecked ship. Their flashlights illuminate the vessel's dark corridors and crevices.

Asher checks his watch.

INSERT - DIVE WATCH

3:40

BACK TO SCENE

Asher pulls his gaze from his watch. He waves for Sean to follow him out of the ship.

41   EXT. UNDERWATER - THE MIZPAH WRECK - DAY   41

Once outside, Asher looks at his watch again. He gestures for Sean to stay, then dares to go back inside the ship!

Sean looks at Asher utterly shocked, but doesn't dare to follow.

42   INT. UNDERWATER - THE MIZPAH WRECK - DAY   42

Inside, Asher scours the ship for the clue, paddling this way and that, searching... searching...

43   EXT. DOCKS - DAY   43

Val GASPS when she sees Pauly return to the docks without Asher and Sean.

She paces nervously, thinking what to do. She eyes a jetski rental, deliberating.

44   INT. UNDERWATER - THE MIZPAH WRECK - DAY   44

At last, Asher spots something carved into the ship's inner wall.

INSERT - MIZPAH'S WALLS

The word "MUCK" carved in the metal hull. Next to that are carved the initials "JT."

BACK TO SCENE

Asher smiles.

45   EXT. UNDERWATER - THE MIZPAH WRECK - DAY   45

Asher returns to Sean and gives him a thumbs up.

46   EXT. DIVE SITE - DAY   46

            Above the waves, Asher and Sean emerge. Tearing off their
            goggles, they sigh in relief.

                          SEAN
                  Did you find the clue?

                          ASHER
                  Yes. Where's Pauly? And the other
                  ship?!

                          SEAN
                  Uh oh.

47   EXT. OCEAN - DAY   47

            Val skids her jetski carefully across the waves. Each bump
            terrifies her and she's afraid to go too fast.

            She stops the jetski.

                          VAL
                  C'mon, c'mon! Okay... three, two...
                  one.

            She revs the engine as fast as it'll go. She SCREAMS as the
            jetski flies off, into the distance.

48   EXT. DIVE SITE - DAY   48

                          SEAN
                  We're dead.

                          ASHER
                  We're not dead, we need to swim
                  back to shore.

                          SEAN
                  How far is it?

                          ASHER
                  A mile and a half.

                          SEAN
                  I'll drown before we get there!

                          ASHER
                  Shut up! We gotta lose our scuba
                  gear. Can you unbuckle your tank?

                         SEAN
             Wait...

On the horizon, a jetski speeds toward them. It's Val!

                         VAL
             Climb on! I don't wanna be out here
             any longer than I need to be.

49   EXT. OCEAN - DAY   49

Val pilots her jetski across the ocean at lightning speed.
She bolts over waves and troughs while Asher and Sean cling
tightly to her and each other.

50   EXT. INTRACOASTAL WALKWAY - DAY   50

Asher, Sean, and Val come to the long walkway that overlooks
the Palm Beach Intracoastal Water Way. Boats sail gently by
and the sound of the tide spashes against the seawall.

Asher paces back and forth, thinking. Sean stands patient and
still, speaking with Asher. Val takes a seat on the seawall
and searches for something on her phone.

                         SEAN
             By the way, thanks Val. Aren't you
             thankful, Asher.

                         ASHER
             Yeah--thanks.

He keeps pacing, trying to focus.

                         VAL
             Don't mention it.

She keeps fiddling with her phone.

                         SEAN
             So what'd you say the next clue
             was? Muck or something?

                         ASHER
             Just Muck. Then the initials again.
             JT.

                         SEAN
             Glad we dove 70 feet a mile
             offshore to see the word Muck.

                    ASHER
               (still pacing)
          Muck is a type of soil, usually
          from a drained swampland.

                    SEAN
          Sounds like most of Florida.

                    ASHER
          There's gotta be something else to
          it.

                    VAL
          Got it!

Val stands and joins the boys, who look to her phone.

                    VAL (CONT'D)
          It's Pahokee. Look, "Locals call
          Pahokee The Muck, because of its
          mineral-rich soil."

Asher looks at her, pleasantly surprised.

                    ASHER
          Nice work.

                    VAL
          But what do we do when we get
          there?

                    SEAN
          We don't have the map.

                    ASHER
          What was that first clue? After the
          Mizpah?

Asher and Sean think--they don't remember.

                    SEAN
          Oh! Casino... Queen!

                    ASHER
          Queen's Tower!

Val's confused.

                    SEAN
          Something about the Queen's Tower.

38

                          ASHER
          I'm sure we'll know it when we see
          it.

                                      SMASH CUT TO:

51   EXT. TOWER - DAY   51

      Asher, Sean, and Val stand beside their parked car, gazing at
      A MIGHTY TOWER.

      It is a strange sight indeed, since most of Florida is fairly
      modern. The tower appears medieval, with earthy brown stones
      stacking their way five stories high.

      By contrast, the land around is sheen, green, and absolutely
      flat. A few gardens, groves, and ponds surround the historic
      monument. But even these natural beauties cannot keep ones
      attention from the bold battlement that looms over all.

      Asher parked his car in the oustkirts of the tower, on a
      desolate road shrouded by trees and shrubs.

                          VAL
                     (reading a sign)
          "La Reina del Cielo."

                          ASHER
          Queen of Heaven.

                          SEAN
          You made that up.

                          ASHER
          It's Spanish. It's not that hard.

                          VAL
          So was this place made for a
          Spanish Queen or something?

                          ASHER
          No, this is St. Mary's Church, as
          in Mary, "Queen of Heaven."

                          VAL
          Wasn't Mary just Jesus' mom.

                          ASHER
          In Hebrew culture, the mother of
          the king was queen.

                          VAL
          Huh.

Asher starts toward the tower.

                    SEAN
          Whoa, wait. We can't just waltz in
          there! We need a plan.

                    ASHER
          Well, you got one or what?

52   EXT. TOWER ENTRANCE - DAY   52

Sean and Val move toward the tower's entrance, spotting a few
ARMED GUARDS.

                    SEAN (V.O.)
          We made pretty good time getting
          here. Giacomo might still be
          inside, and we still need his map.

53   INT. TOWER ENTRANCE - DAY   53

The Tower's ground floor is an immaculate lobby. A small
kiosk sits near the front and a series of seats for reclining
and study lay about the rear. TOURISTS meander through the
spectacular space.

Sean and Val split up. Sean finds a corner of the room to
sit. He peruses a brochure, trying to look inconspicuous.
He's semi-disguised with a hat and jacket.

                    SEAN (V.O.)
          He hasn't seen Val. She'll stall
          him and try to take the map.

Val intentionally bumps into Giacomo, who was on his way out
of the tower.

                    VAL
          Sorry, sir. Wait are you Giacomo
          Tonti? The Giacomo Tonti?

Giacomo takes the bait. He smiles.

                    GIACOMO
          You've heard of me?

54   INT. TOWER STAIRWELL - DAY   54

Asher quickly climbs the tower's long, spiral stairs.

> SEAN (V.O.)
> Meanwhile, Asher can climb the
> tower and look for the next clue.

55   INT. TOWER STEEPLE - DAY   55

Asher arrives at the top of the tower. The steeple has four
sides and four windows. Above each window hangs a Latin
phrase.

56   INT. TOWER ENTRANCE - DAY   56

> VAL
> What brings you this way? A book
> signing?
>
> GIACOMO
> (charmed; in a hushed
> tone)
> Nah, not this time. It's a new, uh,
> adventure.
>
> VAL
> Wowza... Tell me all about it!

57   INT. TOWER STEEPLE - DAY   57

Asher searches the tower's peak up and down for any clue. He
looks out the four windows, but sees nothing of note.

58   INT. TOWER ENTRANCE - DAY   58

Giacomo shows Val the map.

> GIACOMO
> It's a trail of riddles. "Climb the
> Queen's Tower, then be prudent."

59   INT. TOWER STEEPLE - DAY   59

PRUDENTIA. A Latin sign, hanging above the south-bound
window. The letter 'A' has a hole in it. Additionally, Asher
notices the sign is crooked.

He takes the sign off the wall and holds it up to the window.
Matching the base of the sign with the distant horizon, Asher
reveals the next clue: The hole in the 'A' aligns with a far-
off railroad!

60   INT. TOWER ENTRANCE - DAY   60

                        VAL
              So what comes next?

Val tries to read the next line, but Giacomo folds the map.

                        GIACOMO
              You'll just have to wait and see.

Giacomo starts to walk away. Sean steps up, not sure what to
do. Val, thinking quick, approaches Giacomo again.

                        VAL
              Wait, can I have a picture with
              you?

                        GIACOMO
              Sure.

They pose as Val goes to take a selfie.

                        VAL
              With the map please, or my friends
              won't believe me.

Giacomo's a bit suspicious, but obliges. He lifts the map
into the frame of Val's photo.

                        VAL (CONT'D)
              One, two...

Past the phone's screen, Giacomo spots Sean. He snaps the map
back down and turns to run away.

But Val, thinking fast, snatches the map from his hand. She
takes off and Sean follows close behind.

                        GIACOMO
              Hey! Stop!

Two guards rush into the room and look to Giacomo.

                        GIACOMO (CONT'D)
              They stole my wallet!

The guards run after Sean and Val. Giacomo exits in another
direction.

61   EXT. TOWER GARDEN - DAY   61

Sean and Val come to a fork in the path. The guards are
following close behind.

> VAL
> Give me the map!

Sean hands Val the map, who immediately tears it into two halves and hands one to Sean.

> VAL (CONT'D)
> Split up!

They dash in opposite directions. The guards split up and follow them.

EXT. TOWER GROUNDS - RUINS - DAY   62

Val sprints into a ruined area. She turns back to see if she's being followed. Nothing yet.

When she turns again, she's spooked by Asher.

> ASHER
> What happened?

> VAL
> Follow me!

They run off as a Guard gives pursuit.

EXT. TOWER GROUNDS - BUSHY GROVE - DAY   63

Val and Asher have a long lead on their Guard, so Val leads Asher behind a thick bush and the two duck for cover.

> ASHER
> (whispering)
> This isn't gonna work.

> VAL
> Shh!

The Guard enters the area. He pauses and glances about the space. He paces toward the bush...

EXT. TOWER GROUNDS - BRICK WALL - DAY   64

The other Guard keeps close pace with Sean, who's jumping over benches and fences to avoid him.

Rounding a corner, he ditches his jacket and hat and walks back the way he came, nonchalantly, trying to appear like a different person.

At first, when the Guard arrives, he overlooks Sean. But when
the Guard spots Sean's jacket and hat by the path, he turns
around to spot him, but Sean's already vanished.

65   EXT. TOWER GROUNDS - BUSHY GROVE - DAY   65

Val and Asher hold their breath as the Guard draws
dangerously close to them. With inches to spare, the Guard
turns and exits the area.

They exhale in relief.

                    ASHER
          What happened?

                    VAL
          Giacomo caught onto us, so I
          snatched it from him and took off.

Val shows Asher her half of the map.

                    VAL (CONT'D)
          Sean's got the other half.

Asher smiles with a hint of flirting. He's impressed, and
Val's growing on him.

                    VAL (CONT'D)
          So what does it say?

The two shimmy close together, still under the bush, as they
read the map.

                    ASHER
          "Climb the Queen's Tower, then be
          prudent." I thought so. "Follow the
          Magician's Trail toward his city."

                    VAL
          What does that mean?

                    ASHER
          Up in the tower, there were four
          windows. Each was a cardinal virtue-
          -Prudence, Justice, Courage, and
          Temperance. "Prudence" faced South
          and pointed to a railroad.

                    VAL
          The "Magician's Trail"?

                    ASHER
Miami's called the "Magic City" for
popping up almost overnight. So,
the "Magician" is probably Flagler
who built the railroad.

                    VAL
So we follow the railroad South.

                    ASHER
Right. Until, "Leave iron for
water."

                    VAL
A river.

                    ASHER
Could be. Let's find Sean.

66   EXT. PARKED CAR - DAY   66

Sean shows up first, totally out of breath. He folds his half
of the map and stuffs it in his pocket. Then Asher and Val
arrive.

                    SEAN
That could've gone smoother.

                    ASHER
We got what we came for.

                    SEAN
Where we heading now?

                    VAL
South. Following the railroad.

                    GIACOMO (O.S.)
Not bad.

Giacomo emerges from nearby with a REVOLVER in his hand!

                    GIACOMO (CONT'D)
Now gimme the map.

He aims the gun at Val.

                    SEAN
Here.

Sean surprisingly steps forward, drawing his half of the map.
It's folded. It could pass for the whole thing, since Giacomo
didn't see them tear it!

                    SEAN (CONT'D)
          Take it. It's not worth it.

Val stays still, catching onto Sean's plan.

Giacomo takes the map. He's about to unfold it when Asher
steps forward.

                    ASHER
          Giacomo. My mother's sick. She
          needs the fountain to heal her.
          Please.

                    GIACOMO
          That's nice.

                    ASHER
          You can have all the glory for
          finding it, I just want a cup for
          her.

Giacomo ignores him.

                    GIACOMO
          Let me see your wallets, too. And
          phones.

One by one, they turn over their belongings.

                    VAL
          You're a monster.

                    GIACOMO
          It's the name of the game.

Giacomo backs away slowly, keeping his pistol aimed at his
three competitors. Once he's a good distance away, he turns
and scurries off.

Val pulls out her half of the map and smirks.

                    ASHER
          Quick, before he realizes.

They pile into Asher's car and drive off.

67   EXT. BAR - DAY   67

Asher's car pulls off the road and into the parking lot of a
rickety, old bar. Meanwhile:

46

                        VAL (V.O.)
          Ya'll bring any snacks? I'm
          starving.

                        SEAN (V.O.)
          Me too.

                        ASHER (V.O.)
          We're almost outta gas. Search the
          car for any loose change.

68   INT. BAR - DAY   68

Asher, Sean, and Val sit at a grungy bar. They each drop a
few bills and a pile of coins on the table.

Sean tallies the money.

                        SEAN
          Twenty bucks. If we use half that
          for gas, then split a
          cheeseburger...

                        ASHER
          This isn't sustainable. We've
          somehow gotta turn this into more.

                        VAL
          How?

                        CARDPLAYER 1 (O.S.)
          Full house!

Asher, Sean, and Val look and see a game of poker played at a
round table nearby. CARDPLAYERS 1, 2, and 3--gruff looking
men with cowboy hats--sit at the table. Cardplayer 1 takes
the winnings of a recent pot while 2 and 3 reset for another
hand.

Val turns back to the boys.

                        VAL
          Let me play.

                        SEAN
          You wanna gamble away our last
          twenty bucks?

                        VAL
          I can do this. Trust me.

                        ASHER
          You've played before?

                         SEAN
                    (to Asher)
          Don't.

Val nods. Asher thinks it over.

                         ASHER
               Play smart.

He hands her the money and smiles at her. She returns a
flirty smile, takes the cash and walks toward the table.

At the poker table, Val, feigning shy, takes a seat.

                         VAL
               Afternoon, sirs. Mind if I join
               ya'll?

Cardplayer 2 scoffs, but 1 invites her to sit down.

                         CARDPLAYER 1
               Please do.

                         CARDPLAYER 2
               A lady, huh?

Asher and Sean take a seat near the poker table. Val plays a
hand in the background while Asher and Sean chat.

                         SEAN
               When did that happen?

                         ASHER
               What?

Sean makes a knowing face and gestures between Asher and Val.

                         ASHER (CONT'D)
               Nothing's happened. We need cash.
               Quick.

Back at the poker table.

                         VAL
               Wowza!

Val wins the pot, scooping up her winnings. Cardplayer 2
frowns.

Asher smiles and looks to Sean. Meanwhile, a new hand begins
behind them.

                         ASHER
               See?

Sean smiles, knowingly.

                ASHER (CONT'D)
     What?

                SEAN
     Nothing.

                ASHER
     <u>What?</u>

                SEAN
     I just never thought I'd see the
     day.

                ASHER
     See what day?

                SEAN
     You like her.

                ASHER
     I don't.

He looks at Val.

                ASHER (CONT'D)
     I don't...

Back at the poker table, Val wins another hand.

                VAL
     Pocket aces!

She moves to swipe the cash off the table, but Cardplayer 2
slaps his hand on hers to stop her.

                CARDPLAYER 2
     Not so fast, little missy.

                VAL
     Excuse me?

                CARDPLAYER 2
     You hustling us. Strange little
     girl walks in here and wins two
     hands in a row.

                CARDPLAYER 3
     Does sound rather unlikely.

                VAL
     I won fair and square.

                    CARDPLAYER 1
          Beginners luck, Phil. Let her have
          this one.

Cardplayer 2 releases her hand.

                    CARDPLAYER 2
          Maybe the little girl can fetch us
          a few beers.

Val inhales to calm herself and stands with her winnings.

                    CARDPLAYER 2 (CONT'D)
          Go on. Fetch.

Val smirks. Then, she PUNCHES HIM IN THE JAW.

Asher and Sean's eyes widen.

                    SEAN
          Oh crap.

Val's got a look of cruel satisfaction, but it quickly fades
after she realizes what she's done.

The Cardplayers stand up. Asher and Sean quickly flock to
Val's side.

                    CARDPLAYER 2
          Why you little!

He lunges at Val but Asher intercepts him. They tussel. The
poker table's turned over--bills and change fly everywhere.

Cardplayer 3 swings his cane at Val's head, but she grabs it
mid-flight and jabs it back in his face. She then sacks him
to the floor!

Once there, she notices all the loose bills and change. She
quickly swipes up as much as she can, stuffing them in her
pockets.

Sean rushes up to Cardplayer 1, who holds up his hands in
surrender.

                    CARDPLAYER 1
          Hey, hey! He had it coming!

Sean turns his attention to Asher, who stumbles into the bar.
Asher spots a beer bottle. Grabbing it, he spins around and
smashes it into Cardplayer 2's head, who falls down,
unconcious.

69   EXT. BAR - DUSK   69

Asher, Sean, and Val bust out of the bar and sprint for their
car.

                    ASHER
               Go, go, go!

They make it to Asher's car and speed away.

70   INT. ASHER'S CAR - DUSK   70

Val finishes counting the cash.

                    VAL
               We've got about two-hundred.

                    ASHER
               Not bad, Val.

                    VAL
               Thank you.

                    SEAN
               Not bad?! She punched a guy!

                    ASHER
               Yeah. And it was a nice shot.

71   EXT. LONG ROAD - DUSK   71

Asher's car continues down the long stretch of road as the
sound of a train echoes nearby.

72   EXT. MOTEL - NIGHT   72

Asher approaches a HISPANIC MAN.

                    ASHER
               Excuse me?

                    HISPANIC MAN
               Si?

                    ASHER
               Me permite usar su telefono?

Hispanic Man looks at Asher, suspicious.

                    ASHER (CONT'D)
          Es para mi madre que esta en el
          hospital.

                    HISPANIC MAN
          Aqui.

He hands Asher his cell phone. Asher dials a number. It
rings, then:

                    MRS. JUNE (V.O.)
          You've reached Gloria June. Leave a
          message and I probably won't get
          back to you.

Asher hangs up calls another number.

                    NURSE (V.O.)
          Palm Beach General.

                    ASHER
          Can I speak with a patient--Gloria
          June? Room 205. It's her son.

                    NURSE (V.O.)
          All patients are sleeping now. Can
          I take a message?

                    ASHER
          Just tell her I love her.
               (beat)
          How's she doing?

                    NURSE
          Not well.

73   INT. MOTEL ROOM - NIGHT   73

Sean and Val are seated at a breakfast table, eating fast
food when Asher enters.

                    SEAN
          Any news?

Asher shakes his head and takes a seat. Sean and Val exchange
glances, they know he's feeling down.

                    VAL
          So, what do you think the fountain
          will be like?

                    SEAN
          Probably like a golden, shiny,
          school water fountain.

Asher chuckles.

                    ASHER
          Some legends make it out to be a
          big roman bath.

                    SEAN
          Sounds unsanitary.

                    VAL
               (sarcastic)
          Like a school water fountain?

                    SEAN
          That, at least, has modern
          plumbing.

                    VAL
          But really, how does it all work?

Asher shrugs, but gives it his best shot.

                    ASHER
          Most say you've just gotta drink
          it. Whether it's a spring, bath, or
          literal fountain, you just take a
          sip and "poof."

                    SEAN
          "Poof," what?

                    ASHER
          Each myth is different. Some say
          you'll live forever, others say it
          heals you if you're sick. One even
          says you'll turn into a baby and
          have to grow up again.

                    SEAN
          That could be fun. "The Boy Genius
          of Palm Beach Elementary."

                    VAL
          If the fountain's ancient, why does
          the map reference a bunch of modern
          stuff?

                    SEAN
          Yeah--like the Mizpah. It's old,
          but not that old.

                        VAL
          Or the railroad?

                        ASHER
          I've thought about that, too. The
          Mizpah was built in the 20's. So
          this map can't be older than that.

                        SEAN
          So it's not a map to the fountain?

                        ASHER
          No, it is. What it means is whoever
          wrote the map, "JT", must've found
          it recently.

                        VAL
          Any idea how you ended up with it?

                        ASHER
          Not yet.

74   INT. MOTEL ROOM - LATER   74

     Val spreads her half of the map out on one of the beds.

                        SEAN
          We've got the bottom half.

                        VAL
          Giacomo can't win.

                        ASHER
          Neither can we. "Pass yellow reeds
          and the great banyan tree...?"

                        SEAN
          We're missing a few clues from the
          top half.

                        ASHER
          We have to find Giacomo again.

                        SEAN
          How?

                        VAL
          Shouldn't be too hard. He'll have
          to find us, too.

                        ASHER
          We keep following the railroad. We
          know that was the next clue.

                         VAL
          Then something about a river.

                         ASHER
             Right.

75   EXT. RAILROAD - DAY   75

Asher and his friends drive alongside the railroad. Their
eyes are glued to the woods around them, looking for any sort
of sign.

76   EXT. RAILROAD CANAL CROSSING - DAY   76

A solitary place, surrounded with pine trees and swampy
woodlands. A railroad crosses over a thin, manmade canal.
Large iguanas line the canal's bed. The sound of a faroff
train echoes in the distance. It's like a Western, but
greener.

Asher, Sean, and Val park their car along a dirt road
adjacent to the railroad. They step out of the car. Val's got
her aviators and rifle equipped.

REVEAL: Giacomo, standing by his own car, parked fifty feet
from Asher's. His revolver is strapped to his side, like a
cowboy. He smiles and spits as Asher and his friends
approach.

Asher's crew stops with a fair bit of distance between them.
The standoff begins.

                         GIACOMO
             Thought I'd find you here.

                         SEAN
             This doesn't have to get ugly.

                         GIACOMO
             Why not?

                         ASHER
             Giacomo, you used to be every kid's
             idol. You taught us all to keep
             exploring. Are you really gonna
             shoot us?

                         GIACOMO
                (nonchalant)
             Yeah. If that's what it takes.

Val loads her rifle.

                    VAL
          Try it, old man.

                    ASHER
          Val, stop!

A beat as Asher redirects his attention to Giacomo.

                    ASHER (CONT'D)
          History's heroes didn't just do
          things, they were things. Don't you
          wanna be remembered as an honorable
          man?

Giacomo laughs.

                    GIACOMO
               (sarcastic)
          Right. I forgot. Colombus was a
          really great guy.

                    ASHER
          Think about Ponce de Leon!

                    GIACOMO
          Him too! They're all jerks.

Asher frowns.

                    GIACOMO (CONT'D)
          Don't take it so personally. Deep
          down, we're all the same.

                    SEAN
          No wonder your show was cancelled.

That hits too close to home for Giacomo.

                    GIACOMO
          You shut your mouth, or you'll be
          first.

His hand drifts to his pistol. Val tightens her grip.

                    VAL
          Don't even think about it!

                    SEAN
          Whoa, whoa!

                    ASHER
          GUYS. C'MON!

A silent beat as things calm down.

                    ASHER (CONT'D)
          Look, I'm sure there's plenty of
          water to go around.

Giacomo laughs.

                    GIACOMO
          I don't want no water.

Sean steps forward.

                    SEAN
          Then the credit. Or glory. Or
          whatever you want. We only need
          some water for his mom.

Asher thinks it over. He's not crazy about that thought.

                    SEAN (CONT'D)
          It's the only way.

                    GIACOMO
          Alright. I get the credit, you get
          some water.

                    VAL
          And we want our phones and wallets
          back!

                    GIACOMO
          Oh, yeah. I, uh, ditched them back
          at the church.

                    VAL
          Jerk.

Giacomo stretches out his hand for a shake.

                    GIACOMO
          We have a deal?

Asher slowly draws near and accepts his hand.

                    ASHER
          What's our next move?

                    GIACOMO
          We follow the canal, till it turns
          to a river about three miles
          downstream. Find a fork, take it
          south.

                    VAL
          Great. More water.

Giacomo pulls out his half of the map.

>   GIACOMO
>   Yours?

Val approaches and unfolds hers. They put their maps
together.

INSERT - COMPLETE MAP

The top half reads: "...Justly sail man's river, then God's
river. At the river split, move prudently." The bottom half,
after the tear, reads: "Pass yellow reeds and the great
banyan tree..."

BACK TO SCENE

>   ASHER
>   "Pass yellow reeds and the great
>   banyan tree, moor in the fire cove
>   by Florida's flame."

Sean perks up at this.

>   GIACOMO
>   That must be a hot water spring.
>   I've been there before--about
>   twenty miles south.

>   VAL
>   Twenty miles?!

>   GIACOMO
>   Yes. So we better get going. You'll
>   need a canoe. There's a rental a
>   few blocks down.

Giacomo waves for the others to follow him. He starts his
walk down from the road to the canal. When Asher moves to
follow, Sean holds him back.

>   SEAN
>   (hushed)
>   He's lying. Florida's flame is a
>   plant--Rhododendron Austrinum.

>   ASHER
>   Maybe he doesn't know that.

>   SEAN
>   Florida doesn't have hot springs.
>   Not in the Everglades--he knows
>   that.

>VAL
What should we do?

>ASHER
What <u>can</u> we do? We follow him for
now. Keep an eye out for that
plant.

>SEAN
Flower.

>ASHER
Whatever!

77   EXT. CANAL - DAY   77

The fatal alliance of four shoves off from the walls of the
canal and begins to paddle away.

RIVER - MONTAGE

BOLD, ADVENTURE MUSIC SWELLS as Asher, Sean, Val, and Giacomo
paddle down the canal.

78   EXT. RIVER - DAY   78

The canal gives way to a natural river. The world becomes
exotic, strange, and uncivilized. The sound of cars and
trains gives way to chirps, cries, and other jungle chatter.

A GATOR'S GREEN EYES peer out of the water.

A panther's ROAR echoes from afar.

At last, they come to A GREAT BANYAN tree that hangs high
over the river.

>GIACOMO
The banyan tree. We'll camp here
for the night.

79   EXT. BANYAN TREE - DAY   79

Giacomo is mooring the kayaks while Asher conferences quietly
with Sean and Val.

>SEAN
(hushed)
We've got the bottom half. We
should leave him.

                         VAL
          At night. Once he's asleep, we
          paddle away.

                         SEAN
          And sabotage his kayak.

                         ASHER
          And if he wakes up, he'll start
          shooting!

                         VAL
          We've gotta get rid of his gun.

Giacomo returns.

                         GIACOMO
                 (to Sean and Val)
          You two, set camp.
                 (to Asher)
          You, kid. With me. Gotta get
          firewood.

                         ASHER
          I'd rather stick with them.

                         GIACOMO
          What? So you three can run off
          without me? Come. Now.

Asher reluctantly follows Giacomo out of the campsite.

80   EXT. BANYAN JUNGLE - DAY   80

       Asher follows close behind Giacomo, eyeing the pistol that
       dangles from his side. Giacomo's eyes scour the ground,
       looking for firewood.

                         GIACOMO
          So where'd you get this map,
          anyway.

                         ASHER
          I don't really know. It's been with
          me since my parents adopted me.
          Maybe earlier.

                         GIACOMO
          Weird.

                    ASHER
          Very. Cause I've obsessed over the
          fountain ever since you... since I
          first learned of Ponce de Leon.

Giacomo stops walking.

                    GIACOMO
          He was a good one. Had a lot of
          firsts.

                    ASHER
          Firsts?

Giacomo faces Asher.

                    GIACOMO
          That's what it's all about. What's
          the sense in finding something
          already found?

Giacomo takes a seat on a log and Asher follows his lead.

                    ASHER
          Will you drink the fountain?

                    GIACOMO
          Sure, but I don't think it'll do
          much. It's a myth. I wanna live
          forever as much as anyone, but
          that's not gonna happen there.

Asher looks down.

                    GIACOMO (CONT'D)
          That's not what you wanted to hear.

                    ASHER
          Yeah, well, you might be wrong.

                    GIACOMO
          I heard a quote once. "You die
          twice. Once when you pass and twice
          when your name is spoken for the
          last time."

                    ASHER
          So?

                    GIACOMO
          There's no life in the fountain.
          Not the sort your looking for. But
          you might "live forever," if you're
          the one who finds it.
                    (MORE)

61

                    GIACOMO (CONT'D)
          People will speak your name
          forever, like Ponce de Leon. If you
          find it first, that is.

                    ASHER
          So you always work alone?

                    GIACOMO
          Until now, apparently. Solo's the
          way to go.

Asher shakes his head with a smile that says, "You do you,
buddy."

Giacomo leans in close, uncomfortably close.

                    GIACOMO (CONT'D)
          Don't tell me you disagree. We both
          wish the other wasn't here.

                    ASHER
          Maybe that's cause you locked us in
          your house and held a gun to my
          face!

Asher stands up and paces away, distancing himself from
Giacomo. But Giacomo pursues him.

                    GIACOMO
          I see it in you. You want to find
          it yourself. You want the "first."
          To look at the fountain and say, "I
          found it on my own. Me!" And then
          to have your name carved among the
          greats: Polo, Vespucci, Ponce De
          Leon.

Asher thinks about what Giacomo just said. He might be right.

                    ASHER
          I'm doing this for my mom.

                    GIACOMO
          No one's saying otherwise. But you
          can want two things at once. Don't
          kid yourself. You want this thing
          just as much as I do.

81   EXT. BANYAN TREE - NIGHT   81

A panther ROARS in the distance, startling Asher, Sean, and
Val. They're gathered around a campfire with Giacomo, who's
unfazed by the sound.

                    ASHER
          Panther?

Giacomo nods.

                    GIACOMO
          Haven't seen its markings, yet. But
          it could be close.

                    SEAN
               (eyeing Asher and Val)
          One of us should stay awake to keep
          watch.

                    GIACOMO
               (sinister)
          I'll do it. Wouldn't want you kids
          falling asleep on the river.

There's a tension in the air. This isn't the way it's
supposed to go.

                    ASHER
          I'll join you.

                    GIACOMO
          Don't worry about it, kid--

                    ASHER
          Wouldn't want the old man up all
          night by himself.

Giacomo frowns.

                    GIACOMO
          Sure. Stay up for all I care.

                                        FADE TO:

82   EXT. BANYAN TREE - LATER   82

Time fades by. Sean's the first asleep.

Giacomo tends to the fire while Val sits with her rifle in-
hand. She eyes him like a hawk.

Asher studies the map, sitting with his back to a tree, but
his eyes are heavy. He tucks the map inside his jacket
pocket.

Val's eyes start drooping lower and lower.

                                        FADE TO:

83   EXT. BANYAN TREE - LATER   83

Sean and Val sleep soundly.

Asher sits with his back to the tree. He tries to stay
focused on Giacomo.

Giacomo sits opposite of him, wide awake, polishing his
pistol.

Asher tries to startle himself awake. He shimmies and shifts.
But soon, sleep overcomes him.

Like a shark, Giacomo immediately moves toward his prey.
Silently, stealthily, he draws near to Asher. Giacomo
crouches down beside him and reaches into his jacket, drawing
out the map.

Giacomo stands quickly to leave but is met with the barrel of
Val's rifle!

                    VAL
          Drop it.

Giacomo is shocked. Sean rises with Val's fire axe. Asher
stands next. It was a ruse!

                    VAL (CONT'D)
          Your gun first.

Giacomo smirks.

                    GIACOMO
          Not bad.

Giacomo puts his hand on his revolver. Val tightens her
stance. Giacomo slowly lowers his gun to the ground and
stands again.

Asher picks up Giacomo's revolver.

                    GIACOMO (CONT'D)
          Not bad at all.

                    ASHER
          Drop the map.

Giacomo begrudgingly obliges. Then he darts into the woods,
slipping into utter darkness.

Val tracks him with her rifle, but Asher stops her.

                    ASHER (CONT'D)
          Let him go.

                              64

Asher sits down and picks up the map. He unfolds it.

> ASHER (CONT'D)
> No.

His expression is pale. Asher shoots up, dropping the map.

INSERT - MAP

It's the top half of the map--the wrong half. Giacomo must have swapped them at the last possible moment.

BACK TO SCENE

> ASHER (CONT'D)
> He's got the bottom half!

84   EXT. BANYAN JUNGLE - NIGHT   84

Asher, Sean, and Val pursue Giacomo's trail into the woods. They scour the horizon with flashlights.

> SEAN
> I can't see anything.

> ASHER
> We have to try. He couldn't have gone far.

> SEAN
> What difference does it make? If we can't see him, he might as well be in another country--

> VAL
> Guys, shut up! Did you hear that?

CREATURE'S POV

Through the low underbrush, we see the shadows of Asher, Sean, and Val searching the woods. We hear the creature's low growl as it slowly draws closer to its prey.

BACK TO SCENE

Asher and his friends shake with terror at the sound.

> SEAN
> Back to the camp?

85   EXT. BANYAN TREE - DAWN   85

         Asher, Sean, and Val enter the camp. Sean investigates the
         grounds, trying to come up with a plan. Val is more
         interested in Asher, who looks away from the camp, absolutely
         hopeless.

                        SEAN
                  He's on foot--his kayak's still
                  here. Doesn't look like he took
                  anything...

         Val watches Asher walk out of the camp.

86   EXT. RIVERBANK - DAWN   86

         Asher takes a seat, facing the river. The rising sun glistens
         in the water's ripples.

         A long beat. Asher takes out his half of the map, crumples it
         in a ball, and tosses it in the river.

         Val gently approaches and sits next to Asher.

                        VAL
                  I'm sorry, Asher.

                        ASHER
                  It's fine.

                        VAL
                  I'm sure your mom will understand.

                        ASHER
                  She doesn't even want this.

                        VAL
                  What?

                        ASHER
                  She doesn't want the fountain. She
                  doesn't want to live.

                        VAL
                  Then why did you come looking for
                  it?

                        ASHER
                  Because I want her to live! And you
                  know what, maybe we should take a
                  few bottles of this stuff. For all
                  of us.

                    SEAN
          Asher, if we go into the jungle
          with no plan, no path, we might
          never come out.

                    VAL
          We'll get lost.

                    ASHER
          Okay so we leave a trail or take
          notes. Something so we don't lose
          our way.

Sean paces away, shaking his head.

                    ASHER (CONT'D)
          What? It's just one more day!

                    SEAN
          You said this was gonna be a road
          trip. Nothing major. Suddenly,
          we're locked in a house,
          practically kidnapped, and Val has
          to break down the door. Next you
          push me off a boat and I'm diving
          with sharks! We canoe miles with a
          psychopath--I'm so sorry I don't
          want to leave my family fatherless!
          I'm sorry I don't want to be eaten
          by a panther!!!

Sean sits and takes a breath.

                    SEAN (CONT'D)
          Okay. I'm good. Sorry about that.

                    ASHER
          You sure?

                    SEAN
          Yeah--just had to get that out of
          my system. Continue.

                    ASHER
          We've at least got the next clue--
          the Florida's flame thing. Give me
          one more day. I really feel like we
          can do this.

Sean thinks it over for a moment.

                    SEAN
          One more day. For your mom.

                         ASHER
                  Yeah, of course.

88   EXT. RIVER - DAY   88

         Asher, Sean, and Val continue their voyage down the river.
         Now their paddle strokes are full of effort and muscle, but
         Asher holds a firm and determined gaze.

         They pass through thick mangrove trees, tall golden reeds,
         and dark, muddy waters. Somehow, this world seems wilder than
         before; the noise of birds and beasts rises, transforming the
         jungle into an otherworldly place.

89   EXT. FLORIDA FLAME COVE - DAY   89

         They paddle toward a shallow cove where Florida Flame
         Azalea's grow.

                         SEAN
                  Rhododendron Austrinum. Florida
                  Flame Azaleas.

         They moor their kayaks and step onto the beach.

                         SEAN (CONT'D)
                  This was our last clue.

                         VAL
                  From here on out, we either get
                  closer or farther.

         Asher approaches the tree line and takes in his surroundings.
         He stares forward in wonder. He looks confused and curious.

                         VAL (CONT'D)
                  You okay?

                         ASHER
                  Something's familiar about all
                  this.

                         SEAN
                  Are you remembering another clue?

                         ASHER
                  Maybe.

         He proceeds into the jungle. Sean and Val follow.

90   EXT. DEEP JUNGLE - DAY   90

JUNGLE - MONTAGE

With Asher leading the way, they pass through thick, wooded
jungle.

They cross a wide open field of brown reeds, bowing with the
wind.

They enter another jungle, thicker than the last. Asher holds
his determined gaze while Sean and Val show signs of
exhaustion.

91   EXT. DEEP JUNGLE CAMPSITE - DUSK   91

Asher and Val are gathered around their new campsite. Sean
returns with a handful of plants.

                    SEAN
          Dinner time!

He distributes the various flowers and herbs.

                    ASHER
          What is this?

                    SEAN
          Food.

He tosses a vibrant flower in his mouth.

                    VAL
          No meat?

                    SEAN
          If you wanna go hunting, be my
          guest. Attract the panther.

Val tries a bite of her greens, forcing herself to swallow.
Asher turns his attention back toward the wilderness.

                    ASHER
          We're close. I can feel it.

Sean rolls his eyes.

                    SEAN
          Right. So what's the plan? We fill
          a canteen for your mom and take it
          home?

                    ASHER
          I was thinking a few canteens.

                    SEAN
          In case it doesn't work at first?

                    ASHER
          No, for us.

                    SEAN
          Huh.

There is a pause. Sean and Val are silent.

                    ASHER
          I mean, what if one of us gets sick
          in a few weeks? We don't wanna hike
          all the way out here again. Right?

                    VAL
          You wanna live forever?

                    ASHER
          You two don't?

Sean shrugs.

                    SEAN
          Not to be all "glass is half empty"
          but it probably doesn't even work.

                    VAL
          I thought this was just about your
          mom.

                    ASHER
          Why can't it be more than that?
          Ever since I was a kid, I obsessed
          over this place because... I'm
          afraid of closing my eyes one day
          and never opening them again. The
          end... the nothingness... it's
          unnatural.

Asher looks to his two friends; their eyes are set on his.

                    ASHER (CONT'D)
          Don't tell me I'm alone on that.

                    VAL
          Everyone feels that way.

> SEAN
> I think it feels unnatural because
> it is. I mean, if it was meant to
> be--if it was a good thing--why is
> it so... awful?

> ASHER
> Exactly! So the only logical thing
> to do is to fight it with
> everything we've got. Medicine,
> fitness, diet, even the fountain!

Silence. Asher notices Val.

> ASHER (CONT'D)
> What?

> VAL
> What would you even do with
> immortality?

> ASHER
> Explore?

> VAL
> What about when everything's been
> found? What then?

Hold on Asher.

92   EXT. ARID JUNGLE - SITE 1 - THE NEXT DAY   92

Asher, Sean, and Val continue their trek through the woods.
The nature that surrounds them looks hollow, wild, and
crooked. An unnatural landscape of death and decay.

CLOSE ON DEEP SCRATCH MARKS, carved into a tree. Asher and
Val pass it by, but Sean holds on it.

> SEAN
> Guys. Guys!

Asher and Val return to the tree.

> ASHER
> Panther.

> SEAN
> We should head back.

> VAL
> You two scared?

                    SEAN
          Of a lion? Yes!

Asher wanders a bit farther forward. He notices something: an
abandoned campsite.

                    ASHER
          Giacomo's been here. We're on the
          right track.

                    VAL
          Maybe the lion got him.

                    ASHER
          I don't see any bones. And the camp
          is fresh.

Meanwhile, Sean pulls out his field guide and flips through
its pages.

INSERT - FIELD GUIDE

Pictures of PANTHERS and their victims. Gruesome images.
Mangled bodies.

BACK TO SCENE

                    SEAN
          We have to leave.

                    ASHER
          Whoa, wait. We're so close to end!

                    VAL
          I've got my gun--we'll be fine.

                    SEAN
          Are you two psychotic?!

                    ASHER
          Sean, for my mom's sake--

                    SEAN
          Don't give me that crap. This isn't
          about her, none of it is!

                    VAL
          I'm sure we can figure out a
          compromise.

                    SEAN
          No. No more compromising. If I let
          this continue, he'll get us all
          killed. I'm done. I'm going home to
          my wife and son.

Sean walks off.

                    ASHER
          Sean!

                    VAL
          Let me talk to him.

95   EXT. ARID JUNGLE - SITE 4 - DAY   95

Val enters an eerily quiet section of the jungle. She's a
little worried, but tries to keep calm and brave.

She quietly draws deeper into the area, practically tip-
toeing. She watches over her shoulder and scours the thick
shrubbery all around her.

Suddenly...

A GROWL!

Val GASPS.

96   EXT. ARID JUNGLE - SITE 3 - DAY   96

Asher hears Val SCREAM, followed by gunshots! He bolts out of
the area.

97   EXT. ARID JUNGLE - SITE 4 - DAY   97

Both Asher and Sean arrive to find Val intact, but with a
long gash in her arm. She's shaking.

Asher draws Giacomo's pistol and stays alert while Sean looks
over her wound.

                    ASHER
          What happened?

                    VAL
          He scratched me but I shot him
          good. Took off that way.

                    SEAN
          C'mon. We're getting out of here.

Cautiously, but quickly, they leave the area.

The eyes of a GREAT PANTHER, shrouded in foliage, track Asher and his friends. Its stomach GROWLS. Then, it darts after them.

98   EXT. ARID JUNGLE - SITE 5 - DAY   98

Asher, Sean, and Val sprint through the jungle as fast as they possibly can.

PANTHER'S POV

The creature flies through the underbrush, blasting through bushes and ferns, pursuing its prey.

BACK TO SCENE

Sean dares a glance behind him. He doesn't see the lion.

                    SEAN
          Where is it?!

                    ASHER
          I don't know!

The Panther appears, running adjacent to them, behind a few rows of trees. It's trying to cut them off! Sean sees him and points.

                    SEAN
          There!

Asher, without stopping, shoots wildly in the direction of the beast.

It vanishes.

                    VAL
          Did you hit him?!

                    ASHER
          I hope so!

PANTHER'S POV

Now the lion tracks them from behind. He's far-off, but gaining speed.

BACK TO SCENE

Sean spots the lion again.

                         SEAN
              Behind us!

Without stopping again, Asher shoots wildly at the lion, but
nothing comes out--he's out of ammo.

99   EXT. ARID JUNGLE - RIVER - DAY   99

Miraculously, they come to a river.

                         SEAN
              Quick! Through the river!

                         VAL
              Watch for gators!

They leap into the river and cross it with all the force they
can muster.

Practically washing ashore, Asher, Sean, and Val gasp for
air, catching their breaths.

Asher looks to the other side of the river.

                         ASHER
              He's gone.

The Panther is nowhere in sight. The jungle is calm and quiet
again.

Sean looks to Val's wound, which still gushes blood. He pulls
out his first aid kit and patches her wound.

                         SEAN
              This is bad.

                         VAL
              I'll be fine.

                         SEAN
              It might be infected from the
              river.

                         ASHER
              Will the bleeding stop?

Sean takes another look at her arm.

                         SEAN
              It should. But she needs a
              hospital. Right away.

Asher's torn.

                    SEAN (CONT'D)
          Asher, we have to leave.

                    ASHER
          Alright. Let's go.

They glance around themselves.

                    SEAN
          Uhh... do you know where we are?

                    ASHER
          Not a clue. But this does look
          familiar.

                    SEAN
          Of course it does. It looks like
          the other hundreds of acres of
          jungle we just came from!

Asher stands and gestures to the jungle ahead.

                    ASHER
          C'mon.

                    SEAN
          Why that way?

                    ASHER
          It's this way. I know it.

                    SEAN
          How could you possibly "know it?"

                    ASHER
          Would you rather go back across the
          river and be lion food?

Sean and Val begrudgingly follow Asher away from the river
and into the jungle once more.

100   EXT. HEART OF JUNGLE - DAY   100

They come to a misty clearing. At once, their senses are
seized by the peculiar place.

MYSTERIOUS, HOPEFUL MUSIC builds. Mist swirls about their
feet. Rays of light pierce through the jungle canopy,
streaming spotlight beams across the forest floor.

                    VAL
          What is this place?

> ASHER
>> This is it.

We hear a TRICKLING OF WATER as our heroes draw deeper into the shrouded plain. At last, THE FOUNTAIN is revealed. The ancient stone pillar still pumps water slowly out its peak, into its bowls, and overflows into the pond below.

By its side, stands the Guardian--the venerable vanguard of the mythical waters. He is young, but stern, like a great banyan tree.

Asher, Sean, and Val cautiously approach the Guardian and his pool. At length, they come near to the man.

> GUARDIAN
>> (grand)
>> At last. Welcome.

Nearly falling to his knees, Asher gazes at the specter in wonder.

> ASHER
>> What are you?

> GUARDIAN
>> (loosening up)
>> Guardian of the Fountain of Youth.
>> Figured that was obvious...

> ASHER
>> Are you God?

Guardian rolls his eyes and exhales.

> GUARDIAN
>> Let's start over.

He morphs. His shadowy appearence transforms into a perfectly normal man. He stretches out his hand for a shake, smiling.

> GUARDIAN (CONT'D)
>> Hi.

Asher, bewildered, cautiously extends his hand. The Guardian shakes it firmly.

> GUARDIAN (CONT'D)
>> Let's get started.

The Guardian walks behind the fountain and, reaching down, produces an elaborate flagon.

                    GUARDIAN (CONT'D)
          I've been waiting for you.

                    ASHER
          For me?

                    GUARDIAN
          Umm, yeah. That's what I said.

                    ASHER
          I don't understand.

                    GUARDIAN
          Yes you do.

He hands Asher the flagon.

                    SEAN
          Maybe he means--

                    GUARDIAN
          Ah, ah! Let him figure it out.

                    ASHER
          You knew I was coming.

The Guardian nods.

                    ASHER (CONT'D)
          How?

                    GUARDIAN
          You already know the answer.

                    ASHER
          No I don't, just spit it out,
          already!

The Guardian stands again.

                    GUARDIAN
          No! I don't want to ruin all the
          fun. This is my favorite part,
          after all. It only comes once every
          eighty years or so. But you're here
          earlier this time.

Asher's starting to get it.

                    ASHER
          You mean...

                    GUARDIAN
          You've left and you've come again.

                    ASHER
I've been here before.

                    GUARDIAN
Yes, but say it with confidence!
You've been here before. Good. But
you already knew that, deep down.
These woods are familiar to you.
You've walked this path before.

                    ASHER
Who am I?!

The Guardian smiles.

                    GUARDIAN
Juan Ponce de Leon.

Val and Sean drop their jaws. Asher's shocked too, but in a
different way--in the way of revelation, or nostalgia. Like
an old wound resurfacing.

                    GUARDIAN (CONT'D)
That face never gets old.

                    ASHER
How many times have I been here?

                    GUARDIAN
This is your eighth time. Five-
hundred years ago, nearly to the
day, you found this place and drank
these waters, turning young again.
So the cycle continued for half a
millennium.

                    SEAN
So when you drink the fountain, you
become a kid again?

                    GUARDIAN
See for yourself.

The Guardian waves his hand. The mist beside the fountain
clears, revealing a set of adult clothing. Giacomo's
clothing.

                    VAL
Is that... Giacomo?

Out of the clothing shimmies an infant, BABY GIACOMO, crying
and wailing.

                    VAL (CONT'D)
          Oh my goodness!

Val picks up the baby and wraps him in Giacomo's old
clothing.

                    VAL (CONT'D)
          What will happen to him?

                    GUARDIAN
          He'll grow up again. Any memories
          from his past life will seem like a
          dream.

                    ASHER
          How did I find this place eight
          times? Did you send me a letter
          each time?

                    GUARDIAN
          Most times it was your gut. Or
          memories from your past lives. Hard
          to tell the difference sometimes.

                    SEAN
          That's how we found it without a
          map.

                    GUARDIAN
          As to the letter, I didn't write
          it.

                    ASHER
          Who did?

                    GUARDIAN
          Who do you think?

Asher thinks for a moment.

                    ASHER
          I did. My past self. And...

He thinks again, straining to remember something.

                    ASHER (CONT'D)
          And I wrote more than one.

                    GUARDIAN
          Excellent work.

The Guardian produces another MYSTERIOUS LETTER from his
cloak and hands it to Asher.

                        VAL
          Aren't you going to read it?

Asher's face stays frozen ahead.

                        GUARDIAN
          He already knows what it says.

                        SEAN
          Well I for one would like to know.

Sean takes the letter from Asher and opens it. Val comes to
his side and the two read it together.

                        JOSHUA THANE (V.O.)
          May 13, 1996.

CLOSE ON ASHER.

                                             FADE TO:

101   EXT. HEART OF JUNGLE - DAY (1996)   101

CLOSE ON JOSHUA THANE, 60s-80s, Asher's past self. He stands
by the fountain, in the same position we just left Asher.

                        JOSHUA THANE (V.O.)
          I hope you enjoyed your adventure
          and I trust the clues I left you
          were not too challenging. We've
          been to this place seven times now.
          We've had seven lives, but we
          haven't used a single one of them.

Joshua takes a seat and pulls out a pen and paper. He begins
writing.

                        JOSHUA THANE (V.O.)
          We've wasted our time searching for
          this place, longing for eternity.
          We've never settled down, had a
          family, and done the things life
          was meant for. Our fear of death
          has kept us from life. Only now, at
          the end, have I realized this. So,
          I implore you to leave this place
          forever and spend your life
          searching for meaning in death
          rather than a way to avoid it.

Joshua takes the Guardian's Flagon and dips it into the
fountain's lowest bowl. He holds the cup to his lips.

                              JOSHUA THANE (V.O.)
                         Eternal life is not for these
                         waters to grant.

CLOSE ON JOSHUA THANE.

                                                    FADE TO:

102   EXT. HEART OF JUNGLE - DAY (2021)   102

CLOSE ON ASHER, staring into the fountain's waters.

                              GUARDIAN
                         (playful)
                    What to choose? What to choose?

                              SEAN
                    Asher, c'mon. Let's go.

Asher doesn't budge. He holds a hard gaze on the fountain.

                              VAL
                    Asher, please.

                              SEAN
                    Let's take some back to your mom
                    and then she can decide.

                              GUARDIAN
                    Not if he drinks it, first.

Asher is literally enchanted by the fountain. His eyes, his
soul, his essence is lost starting at the swirling waters.

                              VAL
                    What have you done to him?

                              GUARDIAN
                    Nothing. This is his own doing.

All sounds fade away.

On and on the water pours and drips down the length of the
fountain, over its lip and into the pond below.

Asher's eyes trace the water, fixated. On and on it goes.

Without breaking eye-contact with the fountain, Asher grabs
the elaborate flagon seated in the earth and holds it to the
fountain's largest bowl.

We see Asher's eyes. The water. The flagon.

Asher dips the cup into the water, filling it to the brim.

We see his eyes. The water. The flagon.

Asher lifts the cup to his lips.

Eyes. Water. Flagon.

Suddenly, he drops the cup. The water rushes out of it and sinks into the earth.

The enchantment ends. Asher is himself again. He backs away, shaking off the strange feeling. He takes a moment to breathe and collect himself.

>   VAL
>   You okay?

>   ASHER
>   Yeah. Let's go.

>   SEAN
>   Go? What about your mom?

>   ASHER
>   She doesn't want it. And neither do
>   I.

The Guardian smiles. His countenance is fully serious now; no hint of jokes or cynicism.

>   GUARDIAN
>   Well said, Juan Ponce de Leon.
>   Follow the setting sun.

Suddenly, miraculously, the Guardian fades into oblivion.

Asher, Val, and Sean back away--startled.

Then, the ground trembles. Vines, weeds, and all sorts of vegetation seize the fountain, choking it in greenery. Soon, the fountain is completely overgrown and appears as Roman ruins.

Its waters stop flowing.

Together, Asher, Sean, and Val--still holding Baby Giacomo, leave the site. As they depart, the ruins of the fountain fade into a thick fog.

>   FADE TO:

83

103   EXT. ARID JUNGLE - DAY   103

    On foot, they pass through the thick, wooded jungle.

    Next, they cross the wide open field of brown reeds.

104   EXT. RIVER - DAY   104

    They paddle their kayaks peacefully down the river.

105   INT. ASHER'S CAR - DAY   105

    Sean, Val, and Baby Giacomo (still in Val's arms) are fast
    asleep. Asher drives the car, awake, but exhausted. He seems
    lost in thought.

106   INT. HOSPITAL HALLWAY - DAY   106

    Asher walks to his mother's room.

107   INT. HOSPITAL ROOM - DAY   107

    Asher enters. Mrs. June smiles wide--love is written all over
    her face. She turns back to her book and rolls her eyes.

                        MRS. JUNE
                  (feigning disgust)
          Oh, it's you.

                        ASHER
          Hey, ma.

    He takes a seat next to her.

                        ASHER (CONT'D)
          What're you reading?

                        MRS. JUNE
          I don't have the time or the
          crayons to explain it to you.

    She smiles, amusing herself.

                        MRS. JUNE (CONT'D)
          How was your trip?

                        ASHER
          Fun. Really fun. But I should've
          been here.

Mrs. June eyes him suspiciously. He's changed.

> MRS. JUNE
> Flattery won't earn you a place in
> my will. But, I'm glad you're here.

> ASHER
> Anything I can do for you?

> MRS. JUNE
> I've always wanted a butler! Well,
> let's see...

108   EXT. HOSPITAL - DAY   108

Asher returns to his car, where he finds Val (and Baby
Giacomo) waiting for him. Val's arm has a bright new patch on
it.

> VAL
> She doing alright?

> ASHER
> Same as always. Your arm?

> VAL
> Great. It wasn't as bad as it
> looked.

> ASHER
> Good, good.

An awkward beat. A romantic tension--neither wants to say
goodbye.

> ASHER (CONT'D)
> So, uh, what should we do with him?

> VAL
> I can take care of him. For now.

> ASHER
> Sweet. That's great.

Another awkward beat. Asher works up the courage to say--

> ASHER (CONT'D)
> You know, I could help you with
> him. If you wanted.

Val blushes and smiles.

                    VAL
          That'd be great. Not sure an
          orphanage would take a fifty-year-
          old man, anyway.

                    ASHER
          Who better to raise a him than a
          five-hundred-year-old?

Val shakes her head, smiling.

                    VAL
          That's so weird.

109   INT. HIGHSCHOOL CLASSROOM - ONE YEAR LATER   109

                    ASHER
          The Fountain of Youth.

Asher's teaching his class again.

                    ASHER (CONT'D)
          El Dorado. Atlantis. Troy. Flat-
          Earth theory!

A few students chuckle.

                    ASHER (CONT'D)
          History is full of legends. "Are
          they real?" They're all real, in a
          way. They teach us about humanity.
          About ourselves. Greed, glory,
          fate, eternity. If we stop
          listening, like Justin, here--

JUSTIN's asleep. Asher snaps in his ear, waking him up,
evoking more laughs.

                    ASHER (CONT'D)
          If we stop listening to them, we
          stop growing. And if we stop
          growing, we'd be like... I don't
          know. Dirt or something.

A few more laughs as Anna raises her hand.

                    ASHER (CONT'D)
          Bathroom?

She nods and he gestures to dismiss her. The bell rings and
students start to shuffle out.

>   ASHER (CONT'D)
>   See ya'll tomorrow! Have a
>   fantastic day.

He turns to grab his notes from the lectern when his student,
Cody, approaches him.

>   ASHER (CONT'D)
>   Yes, Cody.

>   CODY
>   That was a pretty cool lesson, Mr.
>   J.

>   ASHER
>   Thanks, buddy.

>   CODY
>   Do we have an archaeology club
>   meeting this week?

>   ASHER
>   Thursday--right after school.

>   CODY
>   Sweet. I'll be there.

Asher's phone buzzes; it's a call from Val. He waves bye to
Cody, then raises the phone up and answers the call.

>   ASHER
>   Hey, you. We still on for tonight?

Asher rushes around the class, gathering his belongings.

>   ASHER (CONT'D)
>   You got a sitter for Kenny?

He steps out of the room.

110   EXT. SCHOOL - DUSK   110

Asher exits the school and moves quickly toward the parking
lot. He's still on the phone with Val.

>   ASHER
>   See you in a bit.

He hangs up and enters a car. Sean's sitting in the driver's
seat.

>   ASHER (CONT'D)
>   That's your disguise?

                    SEAN
          Oh, sorry.

He puts on a hat and sunglasses.

                    SEAN (CONT'D)
          Better?

                    ASHER
          Better. Camera?

                    SEAN
          Check.

Sean lifts a photo-camera into the frame.

                    ASHER
          Flowers.

                    SEAN
          Check. Callicarpa Americana.

                    ASHER
          Nice. Edible?

Sean nods.

                    SEAN
          Oh, and the, uh--

                    ASHER
          Right.

Asher searches his pockets and produces an engagement ring
box! Sean looks at the ring, impressed and excited for Asher.
Asher gazes at the ring. A new confidence settles over him.

                    ASHER (CONT'D)
          Check.

We see the car pull away from the school and drive into the
setting sun.

                                        FADE TO BLACK.